Angel Secrets

Angel Secrets

Stories Based on Jewish Legend

BY MIRIAM CHAIKIN

ILLUSTRATED BY LEONID GORE

Henry Holt and Company ✦ New York

Henry Holt and Company, LLC
Publishers since 1866
175 Fifth Avenue
New York, New York 10010
www.henryholt.com

Henry Holt is a registered trademark of Henry Holt and Company, LLC
Text copyright © 2005 by Miriam Chaikin
Illustrations copyright © 2005 by Leonid Gore
Distributed in Canada by H. B. Fenn and Company Ltd.

Library of Congress Cataloging-in-Publication Data
Chaikin, Miriam.
Angel secrets: stories based on Jewish legend / Miriam Chaikin;
[illustrated by] Leonid Gore.—1st ed.
p.   cm.
Includes bibliographical references (p.).
ISBN-13: 978-0-8050-7150-4 / ISBN-10: 0-8050-7150-4
1. Angels (Judaism)—Juvenile literature. 2. Legends, Jewish—Juvenile literature.
3. Midrash—Juvenile literature. I. Gore, Leonid. II. Title.
BM645.A6C43 2006   296.3'15—dc22   2004054062

First Edition—2005
Printed in China

1 3 5 7 9 10 8 6 4 2

The book is for my nephew

Michael L. Pearl

—

The angels are for

Nina Ignatowicz

—M. C.

Contents

About the Stories

Midrash, a Hebrew word meaning "search and explain," is a type of story introduced by ancient rabbis to answer questions in the Bible, such as *Where is God? What is Heaven like? Where is it? Who are the angels?* The rabbis searched and found answers in the Bible itself, whose pages, they believed, contained all answers to all questions.

They passed the answers to their students. Students repeated the stories, adding details of their own. Storytellers retold them, weaving in elements of folktales and fairy tales, of legend and mystical thought, creating ever more stories. Over time, with story added to story, a vast library of *midrashim* arose, and became known collectively as *Midrash*.

The stories in this book are based on various *midrashim,* such as the following:

- *There is no blade of grass that does not have an angel that "strikes" it and tells it how to grow.*
- *God set up patterns and systems of all existence in such a way that all are interconnected.*
- *God's decrees are translated into action through angels.*

Like other storytellers, I have added details of my own to the stories, and I too have invented dialogue.

Introduction

"The kingdom of heaven resembles an earthly kingdom."
—Rabbi Moshe Chayim Luzzatto

Before God made our world, he made many worlds. He examined each one, testing it for goodness, for wholeness. Were there enough parts? How did each part work alone? How did it work with other parts? Was there a sufficiency of beauty? Order? Color? Harmony?

"This one does not please me," he said, casting away each world.

Then he made our world, with rivers, sweet-smelling plants, fruit-bearing trees, flying and creeping creatures, and two humans to fill it with people and take care of it. The world hummed with order and was good. If later some small lack or crack should show itself, the humans, whom he had made as thinking creatures, could repair it.

"This pleases me," he said, keeping our world.

Above our world he placed lights—sun, moon, planets, galaxies, and countless millions of stars—each shining down on our world, each point of light to be a guard or guide for living things in our world.

Now, God so liked our world and its features, he made above it a world for himself and his angels, helpers he had made for himself—countless millions of them. So numerous were they, he divided them into types, classes, and stations.

His world, Heaven, was so vast, he divided it into seven parts. Each realm of Heaven had chambers and workshops, caves and coves, palaces and halls, and secret gates and steps that led to places hidden even from most angels. The Heavens numbered seven, but, like the five fingers of a hand, each was part of a whole—of God's Heaven.

And God? He is in the highest Heaven, the Seventh Heaven, hidden by the Holy Curtain, where his main angels—Cherubim, Seraphim, Archangels (among them, a troublemaker), along with thousands of assistants, keep him company. The great Choirs, each with angel Singers and Musicians, are also there. Though the Seventh Heaven is far from us, God is close. For his glory radiates through the Holy Curtain, filling all heavens with an amber glow that travels down, down—through the world of lights—on down to our world. The amber glow is a link to our world. Some people can see it; some only sense it; some do not know it is there.

God made many links. For he did not make the two worlds to be strangers to one another, one above, one below, each alone. He made them to be aware of each other and established links between them for the purpose.

Divine sparks that fell from him as he worked to make our worlds are another link. These sparks that fell on stones, fields, seas, and mountains are still here.

He created classes of angels to be active in the affairs of our world—Guardians, Messengers, Earth Walkers, Alphabet angels, Lawyers, Angels of Forgetfulness, and Scribes.

Souls, too, are a link. Souls dwell in the Palace of Love, in a secret corner of Heaven. When a baby is born, God selects a soul and inserts it into the infant's body. When the body becomes aged and leaves this world, the soul returns to the Palace of Love until it is needed again.

The Prayer Path—the invisible corridor between Heaven and earth on which prayers travel when humans speak to God—is also a link. Another is the River-of-Angels, whose story will soon be told.

The angel closest to God in the Seventh Heaven is Raziel. This is not because he loves her most; God loves all his angels equally. In the beginning, when he created angel classes and gave out assignments, all angels went to their stations, to take up their duties. One angel remained behind.

"Why do you not leave with your group?" God asked.

"I have not been assigned to a group, Holy One," she said, using the angels' name for God.

"You will sit outside the Holy Curtain," God said.

This is how she came by her station—and her name. In Hebrew, *raziel* means "hears God's secrets."

And there she sits, outside the Holy Curtain, seeing and hearing all—or almost all—happy to bask in God's Glory. She is the only angel who keeps her place when other angels change stations.

And now was such a time. Heaven filled with the soft flap of angel wings and the sweet murmur of angel talk as angels left one station to take up duties in another. It was the time for a new Choir to assemble and sing songs of love and praise to God.

Raziel watched Singers arrange themselves in rows, by voice type, and Musicians take places around them. The Choir leader dipped into the store of hymns and chants and made a selection. Raziel loved to hum along quietly to herself as the Choir sang.

At a signal from the leader, Heaven filled with the sweet sound of angel voices singing *"How great, beloved, are your works"* as Musician angels, accompanying them, made harp- and bell-like sounds with their lips.

Bathed in a radiant glow outside the Holy Curtain, Raziel hummed along.

Angels of Forgetfulness

"Babies are born knowing everything."
—Various traditional sources

⌒

Raziel greeted the Wheel angels rolling by on their way to perform some duty. Flame angels leapt and collapsed, leapt and collapsed, as they passed. She glanced up at her favorite link to earth—what she thought of as the River-of-Angels. This river held not water but a dense stream of angels flowing endlessly to earth and back again. Some called them Baby angels, but that was misleading. Angels have no age; they are not born and do not die. The Holy One creates them as and when he needs angels.

Their official name—Angels of Forgetfulness—grew out of the duty they performed on earth—the Birth Ceremony.

Raziel thought back to the time before the Birth Ceremony existed. When the Holy One first created humans in his image, he filled the minds of infants with all knowledge and an understanding of seventy languages. As time passed, he came to regret the plan.

"It is not good, this thing I have done," he said to Archangel Gabriel as he watched humans develop. "They have knowledge but fail to walk in my ways. Too often, they turn away from acts of loving kindness. Too few of them care about justice and mercy. Too many are petty, cruel, and given to telling lies."

"And your wish, Holy One?" the archangel asked.

"Let us erase knowledge from infant minds. As they grow and mature, perhaps their hearts will teach them goodness. Perhaps the sting of pain and disappointment will teach them mercy."

"I can introduce a Birth Ceremony to accompany the act, Holy One," Gabriel said. "But as infants are born every moment, there will be a need for a new class of angels."

"So be it," the Holy One said, creating millions of angels for the purpose.

Gabriel addressed the group. "You are Angels of Forgetfulness," he said.

"And our duties?" asked one.

"You will assemble in a column, fly to the Love Chamber, take from there a strand of God's love, and fly down to earth through the world of stars.

"One by one, wherever a baby is being born, you will drop from the column—"

"Leave the column?" said an angel.

Gabriel was used to the questions of new angels. "The column will close around you," he said. "You will await the baby's birth. When it comes, you will touch the strand of God's love to the infant's upper lip, just under the nose. The dent you leave will erase all knowledge and remain as a symbol of your visit."

"And when it is done?" an angel asked.

"Rejoin the stream of angels, and return," Gabriel said.

Raziel, her eye on the flow of angels, sat up with a start. She had seen a gap between two angels, an unusual sight—a speck of space, thin as an eyelash, but a gap nevertheless. She was not the only one to see it. She heard the Holy One say, "It is the work of Azaz. Send Kasriel to chastise the mischief-maker."

Raziel sent a thought to Angel Kasriel to come, and he appeared.

"*Hineni,* I am here," the angel said.

"There is a gap in the River-of-Angels," Raziel said. "The Holy One sees it as the work of Azaz."

"One of the Two Hundred," Kasriel said, using Heaven's name for jealous angels the Holy One had long ago expelled from Heaven. The Holy One had had reason to do so: When he looked over the world he had made—lands, seas, night, day, plants, trees, flyers, creepers—he found it incomplete. There was no one to enjoy the marvels and wonders he had made. "Come," he said to the angels. "Let us create humans."

The thought greatly disturbed one archangel, who on earth would later become known as Satan. He called together two hundred of his followers and stirred them up. "We angels are the highest form of creation," he said. "If he creates humans in his image, they will become highest. We will lose our importance."

The followers mumbled agreement.

"I will speak against the idea," the archangel said, and went to protest.

"The world has enough creatures," he said to the Holy One. "Fish fill the seas, fowl fill the air, every manner of beast hops or crawls or roams over the land. For each creature, you have provided food to eat. Nothing more is needed."

Satan had forgotten his place. It was not for him to decide if the world lacked something or didn't. It was God's world. He made it, and he could do with it— and with Satan and his followers—as he pleased. For this insolence, the Holy One expelled the lot of them from Heaven. They scattered over the face of the earth, preaching and practicing evil.

"Yes, one of the Two Hundred," Raziel said, answering Kasriel. "And they are still creating mischief, setting person against person, person against the Holy One."

"But they are not allowed in Heaven," said Kasriel. "How can they cause a gap in the flow of angels?"

"When they were here as angels in good standing, they learned many secrets," Raziel said. "Many, but not all. Go now, Kasriel, and strike order below."

With a single flap of his wings, Kasriel left Heaven; with another, he flew past stars and planets; with a third, he was in the same room with Azaz.

The Two Hundred are masters of disguise, able to make themselves look like anyone or anything. But they are easily detected. Their goatlike feet, which they cannot hide, give them away.

"Why have you disguised yourself as an Angel of Forgetfulness?" Kasriel asked Azaz.

"What makes you think that I am not a true Angel

of Forgetfulness?" Azaz asked, pretending innocence.

"Your felt shoes do not hide the shape of your goat feet," said Kasriel.

Azaz shuffled his feet about, as if to hide them.

"Why have you removed an Angel of Forgetfulness from its place?" Kasriel said.

"What makes you think I have done that?"

"There is a gap. You have left a space."

From the look on Azaz's face, Kasriel saw that the mischief-maker had indeed removed an angel but forgotten to close the gap.

"Move aside," Azaz said, to cover his confusion. "My baby is due at any moment."

"It is not your baby," Kasriel said. "And what is that I see wound around your finger?"

"A strand of God's love," Azaz said, drawing circles in the air with the finger.

Kasriel laughed to himself. The strand of love is sacred. It becomes worthless, an empty thing, when touched by anyone who is not a true angel. But he said nothing. The Two Hundred are braggarts and cannot stand silence. Kasriel waited to hear more.

"Would you like to know how I created the gap?" Azaz asked.

"Well . . . ," said Kasriel.

"I fixed my attention on an angel in the flow. Speaking in the voice of Archangel Gabriel, I said, 'Leave the strand of love and return with me.'"

"And the angel left the strand with you," Kasriel said.

"She did," Azaz said.

"And what do you intend to do now?" asked Kasriel.

"Nothing," Azaz answered.

"Nothing?"

"Nothing."

"You removed an Angel of Forgetfulness—to do nothing?" Kasriel said.

"In this case, nothing is everything," Azaz said. He shook the strand from his finger and let it fall to the ground.

"When this baby comes, nothing will touch its lip. It will keep the knowledge it is born with. The one God in Heaven is too powerful. This baby will be a god in this place, and I will be its creator."

"Fool," Kasriel said. "Does a knowledge of facts and languages make someone a god?"

"With my help, it will," Azaz said.

Kasriel looked at him in disbelief. "Who created you?" he asked.

"God did," Azaz said, giving the only possible answer.

"Will this baby be able to create a gnat?"

"If it keeps the knowledge it is born with."

"Did God create you by reciting a fact or by speaking French?" Kasriel said.

Azaz was silent.

"Or did he create you with the mysterious power that only God possesses, the one God in Heaven, who gives life and takes it away?"

"Step aside," Azaz told Kasriel. "My baby is coming."

Kasriel, losing patience, touched a finger to Azaz's wing, burning a hole there. Azaz let out a harsh sound.

"Go from here," Kasriel ordered. "I will set matters right with Archangel Gabriel."

The Two Hundred are vain about their looks. Muttering under his breath, looking back at the hole in his wing, Azaz slipped away, his felt shoes making a *whooshing* sound as he went.

⁓

Raziel heard the *whoosh*. The sound was known in Heaven and brought a smile to the lips of angels. The sound meant a Satan follower had failed in some act of mischief and was slipping away.

"It is a pleasant sound," she heard the Holy One say.

She smiled to herself, savoring the Holy One's enjoyment, and turned to watch the returning angels. They streamed into the workshop of Ya'asriel, Angel-of-the-Seventy-Pencils, where countless angel Scribes sat at countless long tables, an open book before each. Flying over them, each returning angel announced the birth of a new baby, and the Scribe entered the name in the Book of the Living.

In the Choir loft, Singers, accompanied by Musician angels, began a new round of praise. *"Bring it home to your heart that the Holy One is God in heaven above and on earth below—there is none other,"* the Choir sang.

Raziel sang softly to herself, with the Choir, *"Let the trees clap, let the earth rejoice."*

Alphabet Angels

Raziel heard giggling in the Hall of Alphabet Angels and inclined an ear to listen.

These angels are always giggling. The Holy One made twenty-two platoons of them, one for each letter of the Hebrew alphabet, with countless thousands in each platoon. The angels take up the problems humans face daily or that they create for themselves. The platoons are closely attuned to earth. They quickly feel a tug from below when called. If the problem is with an *animal,* which starts with the first letter of the Hebrew alphabet—*aleph*—an *Aleph* angel will go down. A *Samech* angel goes down to handle a *sneaker* problem. A *debt* problem will reach a *Dalet* angel. Letter angels are cheerful angels and always return to Heaven with a story to tell.

Raziel listened to the story being told. A *Bet* angel had returned from a beehive incident. The fields of the *beekeeper*, a woman, were full of flowering thyme, a favorite food of bees. Her bees had always produced great quantities of honey. Suddenly, honey production had slowed to a trickle.

"Some rich man," the *Bet* angel was saying, "a braggart of a fellow, died and was turned into a bee. He was placed in the woman's hive. While other bees worked diligently, he did no work at all, just flew around bragging about how clever he had been in making money. 'I'm, I'm, I'm, I'm,' he buzzed all day. The bragging distracted the other bees. They began to resent him. Each day a hundred more stopped working."

"What did you do?" asked another angel.

"I gave him the voice of a crow," said the angel. "When he croaked 'I'm, I'm, I'm, I'm,' the other bees laughed. He became too ashamed to speak and now hurries from one worker group to another, trying to make himself useful."

The angels giggled.

Raziel smiled to herself. She watched an *Aleph* angel fly off with other letter angels. *Soon,* she thought, *there will be more stories.*

———

The *Aleph* angel arrived at an apple orchard to find a baffled farm family standing about, looking at their trees. Their apples had always been green. Suddenly, red apples began to appear. The farm family did not know what to make of it.

The angel studied the situation. The green apples were as green as new leaves, bold and firm; the red were smaller, modest. The *Aleph* angel understood: the red apples found the green apples attractive. Their red cheeks were the blush of love.

The angel did not make this known to the farm family. They would not understand. Instead, she whispered a thought into the ear of the young son. "The red apples are after all still apples," she said. "Taste one."

The boy plucked a red apple from a branch and bit into it. "Delicious," he said, and passed it to his sister.

She took a bite. "If anything, the red *is* sweeter," she announced to her pleased parents.

Her mission over, the *Aleph* angel was about to return

to Heaven when she saw a troop of *Vav* angels flying off in all directions. One stopped nearby.

"Where are the others off to?" asked the *Aleph* angel.

"Violence has broken out," the angel answered. "They are rushing to put out this fire, quell that riot, block the paths of wild-eyed people who speak of love and throw stones."

"And you?" the *Aleph* angel asked.

"I am here about a vineyard—or rather two vineyards planted in the same soil," *Vav* explained. "Both receive the same amount of rain. The same sun shines on both. In one, the grapes are plump and sweet-tasting. In the other, the grapes are puny and sour."

"Well, you will know what to do," the *Aleph* angel said, opening her wings. "I have been away from Glory long enough and wish to be back," she added as she flew off.

The *Vav* angel entered the vineyard of sweet grapes, where the vintner family themselves tended the vines, and saw how the family settled vines lovingly over frames, even spoke to them, then went in for their morning meal.

In the vineyard of sour grapes, the *Vav* angel saw hired workers hurry through their tasks, tossing vines about carelessly, letting them fall to the ground to be eaten by insects.

Caring and affection make the difference, the *Vav* angel thought. The angel called to a passing wind to blow open the door of the house so the family could see the careless habits of the workers.

The *Vav* angel thanked the wind. "The family will now know what to do," the angel said, preparing to fly back. But his eye fell on a small cluster of pink flowers growing under a tree. He could not leave the sweet sight and bent to look more closely. *The Holy One's handiwork,* he thought, feeling a burst of love for his Maker. *What wonders he has wrought in the world.*

Strange sounds from a nearby pond interrupted his reverie, and he went to investigate. Rabbi Dov Baer stood listening to a frog. The frog sang, and the rabbi sang after him, trying to reproduce the sound. All angels can turn themselves into anyone or anything. Curious, the angel turned himself into a woodsman.

"Rabbi, why are you here so early in the day, imitating a frog?" he asked.

"The frog is the Holy One's favorite Singer," said the rabbi. "I am trying to learn its song."

The angel was surprised. Here was a human who

knew something about the Holy One that he had not known. The other angels would be interested to hear it.

The rabbi looked up. "I must hurry away now. The sun is showing its face to the world, and my pupils wait for me," he said, rushing off.

The *Vav* angel was delayed yet again. He heard a furious scratching and an agitated mumbling and went to investigate. A boy was groveling under a sycamore tree, pawing the earth like a dog.

"Have you lost something?" the angel asked.

The boy rose. "Before my old father died, he told my mother he had hidden a bag of coins under this tree," he said. "I have been digging and digging and have not found it."

"Are you certain this is the tree?" asked the angel.

"This is the tree," the boy said with confidence.

Lost . . . coins . . . tree—this was not the *Vav* angel's concern. But no angel would walk away from an unexpected human problem.

"I will help you look," said the angel.

Angel and boy lay on the ground and, with fingers and hands, crept along the earth, moving soil aside inch by inch, patch by patch, until they arrived at the edge of the road.

"We have turned much earth and found no bag," said the angel.

The boy looked angry. "My father was not a liar," he said.

Lamed angels answered all *L* calls.

The *Vav* angel had seen *Lamed* angels leaving Heaven. There was sure to be a Locator among them.

"Do not worry," said the *Vav* angel. "Help is on the way.

"Locator, come to my side," the *Vav* angel called with a thought.

A figure appeared. What the *Vav* angel did not know was that the *Lamed* angel had been investigating the doings of this very boy.

"I heard you say your father died," the Locator said to the boy. "When was that?"

"This morning," said the boy.

"This morning?" the *Vav* angel asked, surprised. "And you are not at home mourning for your father?"

The boy looked sheepish. "My mother is mourning," he said. "One family member is enough."

"Let us return to the tree and start again," the Locator said.

All three returned to the tree.

"Show us where you think the bag of coins was hidden," said the Locator.

The boy flung himself upon the ground. "Here! I put it right here!" he said in a frenzy, digging the earth with his fingers.

"Oh! Ow! My finger!" he cried, leaping up suddenly, hopping about in pain, holding up a swollen purple finger.

As a *Lamed* angel, it was a function of a Locator not only to find lost items but also to investigate lies and liars.

"The boy is a liar and a thief," said the Locator. "A donkey driver stopped here to rest and fell sleep. This boy came along, stole the driver's bag of coins, hid it under the tree, and ran from the place, planning to return after the donkey driver had moved on. I woke the driver and caused him to trip as he got up and find his bag of coins."

The Locator turned to the boy. "The bag is with its rightful owner," he said.

"Oh! Ow!" the boy cried, blowing on his finger, now twice the size of his other fingers. "Something bit me. Fix my finger!"

"That is your finger for life," said the *Lamed* angel. "It is the mark of a thief and a liar. Your father died three years ago. Now, go to your old mother and see if you can be of some help to her."

The boy, waving his finger in the cool air, hurried away.

"It is time for me to return," said the *Vav* angel.

"I still have some business here in the vicinity," said the *Lamed* angel, drifting off.

As the *Vav* angel opened his wings to fly up, a *Samech* angel appeared.

"Sparrows again?" the *Vav* angel asked, recalling an earlier visit the *Samech* angel had made to earth. He had gone down to rescue sparrows. A farmer, angry about sparrows nibbling his cherries, had offered hunters money for every pair of birds killed. The *Samech* angel had brought along at the time a strong wind that, with a great gust, had blown the sparrows to safety.

"Sparrows, yes, but in reverse," said the *Samech* angel. "The farmer now wants the sparrows back. His fruit was eaten up by caterpillars. He has seen that sparrows are a farmer's friend. They may nibble a few cherries, but they eat great quantities of harmful insects."

Both angels continued on their way. The *Samech* angel went off to handle the sparrow situation. The *Vav* angel again opened his wings. This time, with nothing to distract him, up, up, up he flew, longing for the Hall of Alphabet Angels and the sweet precincts of Heaven.

Stay, Stone, Stay

*"These are [the angels] whom the Lord
hath sent to walk to and fro through the earth."*
—Zechariah 1:10

In the shack in the poor part of town where they lived, Ora and her mother, Lila, sat crying, wondering who would provide for them now that Ora's father had died.

"How will we get food?" Ora asked.

"I don't know," her mother said.

"This is Angel Goralnik speaking," a voice said.

Ora and her mother looked up but saw no one.

"Where are you?" asked Lila.

"Here," the voice said.

"I don't see anyone," Ora said.

"I didn't come to be seen but to tell you something."

"Yes?" Ora and her mother said in unison.

"You don't have to worry," the voice said. "Go to the backyard and bring from there a stone, beige in color."

"Beige?" Ora asked.

"That's what I said."

An angel was an angel, so Ora hurried out. She soon returned with a stone, beige in color.

"Dry your tears on the stone, both of you—first you, then your mother," the voice said.

Ora and Lila dried their tears on the stone, first one, then the other.

"With this stone, you will always have what to eat. Touch it to the earth and food will grow."

"How is that possible?" asked Ora.

"With us, everything is possible," said Angel Goralnik. "Go and see for yourselves."

Ora and her mother hurried out to the back, touched the stone to the earth, and tall weeds sprang up around the yard.

"This is nice, but it is not food," said Lila.

"This is a fence," the voice said. "Now touch it again."

Ora touched the stone to the earth again, and the

yard became covered with potatoes, parsnips, turnips, onions, carrots, and a tomato vine heavy with tomatoes.

"A blessing!" Ora exclaimed.

"We must thank the Creator," said her mother.

They filled a basket with vegetables, brought it inside, and—peeling, cutting, slicing, chopping—prepared a pot of soup. They left the soup to cook and went out to the woods to show the Creator appreciation of the wonderful world he had made. They walked about, singing to the thistles and grasses, kissing wildflowers, hugging trees.

The rich people living on the hill watched them. "Look at them," they said to one another, laughing. "Stroking trees, talking to birds, smelling plants. Where does it get them?"

Ora and Lila came home before nightfall, and as they ate Lila said, "It is not enough to kiss flowers to show our appreciation to the Creator. We must share the blessings of the earth with others."

From that day on, Ora and her mother spent Fridays cooking and baking. In the afternoon, they went to deliver food to the poor so they and their children would have what to eat on the Sabbath. With a sack of bread slung over her back, Ora smiled. Her curls bounced as she and her mother carried a big pot between them, humming and singing as they went.

Watching them, the laughter of the people on the hill turned sour.

"I smell soup," said one.

"I see bread," said another.

"How does the girl come by such red cheeks when they are so poor?" they asked. "Our children eat meat three times a day and are sickly and pale."

The mystery gnawed at them. So they hired Old Tom—who would do anything for a dollar—to investigate. Friday morning, Tom waited for Ora and her mother to leave with the pot. Then he crept up to the shack, crept in, looked around, and crept out again.

"Nothing there," he reported to the people on the hill. "A pot, two plates, two spoons, forks and knives, candlesticks, and a stone."

"A stone?" they said, smelling something. "What kind of stone?"

"An ordinary stone, like the ones in your backyard and mine," Old Tom said, and put out his hand for the dollar.

The people on the hill never did learn that the stone was not ordinary. But they rid themselves of the mystery.

They stopped watching Ora and Lila and soon forgot about them altogether.

One Friday, when Ora and Lila returned home, they found, sitting at the kitchen table, a man in a white beret wearing small round glasses and chewing on a toothpick. His suit was shiny with wear, and his shirt was frayed. Peeping out from the jacket was an embroidered vest—fancy but not too clean. He sat with one leg over the other. The sole of the shoe in the air had separated from the top and hung loose.

He peered at them over his glasses. "I suppose you wonder who I am." he said.

"The voice is familiar," Ora said.

"I am Angel Goralnik," he said, rolling the toothpick to one side of his mouth.

"I thought all angels were . . . up there," Ora said, looking up.

"I used to be up there," said Angel Goralnik. "Along with Gabriel and Rafael and the others."

"What happened?" Lila asked.

"I wasn't good at it. So they reassigned me."

"Ohhh," Ora and her mother said.

"Don't feel sorry for me. I like my job, walking the earth, meeting people," he said. He cleared his throat and added in a more formal tone, "I have come today because there is something you must do."

"Anything," Ora said. "We are deeply grateful for your help and kindness."

"It's not my help and not my kindness," the angel said. He removed the toothpick and put it in his vest pocket. When he stood, he slapped the loose sole of his shoe on the floor, lining it up with the top.

"Here's what you have to do," he said. "Jerusalem is crying. The city stands empty and alone. The people have fled."

"Oy!" Lila cried, clapping her hands.

"How come?" Ora asked.

"That's where you come in," said Angel Goralnik, sucking on a tooth, trying to dislodge something stuck there. "Take the stone and go to Jerusalem," he said.

Mother and daughter looked at each other.

"How do we get there?" asked Lila.

"Put one foot before the other," Angel Goralnik said.

"Which way is Jerusalem?" Lila asked.

"You don't have to know," said Angel Goralnik. "The stone will take you there."

"But, Angel," Ora said, "what if we lose the stone?"

"You can't lose the stone. It will hang on to you, as

you will hang on to it," he said. "Still, to be on the safe side, sing this song twice a day:

"Honey there is and plenty of milk,
A jewel or two and evenings of silk,
Stay, stone, stay."

He wiped his glasses on the underside of his jacket and disappeared.

"What shall we do?" Ora said to her mother.

"An angel is an angel," Lila said.

"Then let's go," said Ora.

Mother and daughter wrapped pots and dishes in one bundle and candlesticks and Sabbath blouses in another. Ora held on to the stone as she took up a bundle, her mother picked up the other bundle, and both went outside.

"Is Jerusalem to the left or right?" Ora asked.

In answer, the stone pulled Ora away. Lila hurried after her, and the two of them, putting one foot before the other, sticking close to one another, followed the pull of the stone.

On their travels, they wanted for nothing. If they were hungry, there was a tablecloth on the grass with food. If they were thirsty, there was a brook. When night fell, a cloud in the shape of Angel Goralnik's beret appeared and led them to an inn, where a cozy fire crackled in the grate and a clean bed awaited them.

Each morning and evening they sang the stone song:

"Honey there is and plenty of milk,
A jewel or two and evenings of silk,
Stay, stone, stay."

Day after day, the stone pulled them onward, through cities, towns, and villages, past markets and over sands.

One day, the stone stopped pulling. Ora and her mother set down their bundles. They looked about and saw empty streets and empty houses. Shutters hung from broken windows. Grass grew wild between paving stones. In the distance, a coyote howled.

"What is this sad-looking place?" Lila said.

"The angel said the city is crying," Ora said. "It must be Jerusalem."

As she spoke the word, the stone gave a jerk and pulled her away.

"Take the bundles," Ora cried, and reached for her mother's hand. The stone swept up mother and daughter and pulled them along a wall of beige stone, dragging them feverishly, as if it were in search of something, now up, now down. Suddenly, it yanked itself out of Ora's hand, slid into an empty space in the wall, and tucked itself in.

Ora and her mother fell gently to the ground. When they rose and dusted themselves off, Angel Goralnik was standing beside them, nodding at the wall and chewing on his toothpick.

"So that was it!" he said.

"What was?" Ora asked.

"This is the reservoir," the angel said. "The stone was missing. . . ."

"How did it happen?" Ora asked.

Angel Goralnik shrugged. "Who knows," he said. "However it happened, it looks like the water ran out. People had no water, not for themselves, not for their animals, not for the earth. There was no food. One family after another left. Soon the city stood empty."

"You didn't know this?" Ora said.

"I don't know anything and don't need to know," the angel said. "I take my orders from an angel named Kasriel. He tells me what to do, and I do it."

Ora had a sudden worry. "Angel Goralnik," she said, "what will become of us? We no longer have the stone."

"You didn't need the stone. The stone needed you— a pure person," the angel said, and disappeared.

Ora and her mother looked at each other.

"We can't just stand here. There is work to do," said Lila.

They took up their bundles, went into an empty house, and began brushing away cobwebs, sweeping, and dusting. They found some old nails and with a board hammered them flat and nailed in place the shutter that opened on the street. Then they fixed the back shutter, and when they looked out they saw a fig tree full of figs, a pomegranate tree with pomegranates, and dates hanging from a date palm.

Mother and daughter opened their bundles, took out plates, and prepared for themselves a fine meal.

When the rainy season came, rains fell into the reservoir and stayed there. Crows, sparrows, hoopoes, and blackbirds with orange beaks filled the air with joyful sounds. People of neighboring villages came to look, and word spread that the reservoir was filled with water. Farmers returned with their families and planted. Carpenters returned with hammers and nails. Families came with goats, donkeys, and sheep. The air rang with the sound of hammer blows. Soon, sweet-smelling plants covered the ground, children's laughter echoed in the streets, and Jerusalem hummed with the breath of life.

Ora and her mother continued to make soup and bake bread on Fridays to distribute to the poor for the Sabbath. When they returned home, they washed up, put on Sabbath blouses, and spread the table with a white cloth. They lit candles and put on the table, in honor of the song they used to sing, a pot of honey. Then they sat down to a Sabbath meal of roast chicken and a prune and carrot pudding.

As they sat there enjoying their meal, the dancing flames of the burning candles threw a pattern of shapes resembling the embroidery on Angel Goralnik's vest onto the wall.

Sign-Minders

Angel groups flew in neat columns through the amber glow of Heaven on their way to and from assigned tasks. Sweet voices of the Heavenly Choir were ending a round of praise, singing *"Great and mighty, great and mighty are his works."*

When the song was over, a Musician angel approached Angel Raziel.

"Angel Raziel," the angel said, "the First angels, our teachers, tell us stories about beginnings. They say the Holy One made the world below to resemble our world."

"That is so," said Raziel. "The opposite is also true. He so liked some things he had put into that world, he installed them also in our world."

"The First angels also teach that humans strive to be like the Holy One by imitating his kindness and goodness," said the Musician angel.

"And by becoming creators themselves, and creating things to make their world better."

"That is what moves me to speak," said the Musician angel. "The First angels tell us that the Holy One looks now and then at what humans have done, to see if they have created something that might enhance our world."

"He looks," said Raziel, "but seldom does he find something worth importing."

"This leads me to my request," said the Musician angel excitedly. "In our songs of praise, we cover the whole range of musical sound."

"The singing is beautiful," said Raziel. She noticed the hurt expression on the angel's face. "And beautiful are the harp- and bell-like sounds Musician angels make with their lips," she added. "The Holy One takes great pleasure in your music."

The angel flushed with gratitude. "We were wondering—some other Musician angels and myself—if perhaps humans have created a musical sound that would expand our range," he said. "If so, we can bring greater enjoyment to the Holy One."

"That is for the Holy One to say," said Raziel.

The Musician angel took three steps back, bowed, raised his head, and said, "Holy One—"

The Holy One had heard. The Musician angel didn't have to say more.

"I am well pleased with the songs and music you offer," he said. "But satisfy yourselves—go down and see."

The Musician angel signaled his friends and together they flew off.

Raziel noticed a platoon of new angels. The Holy One had only just created them. Angels flying by asked one another, "Who are they?" "What kind are these?"

One of them glided up to Raziel to ask directly. "I have not seen these before," she said, nodding at the newcomers. "Why do they stand unmoving in one place? Why do they show their hands? It is the custom of angels to keep hands hidden under wings."

Other angels gathered around to listen.

"They are newly created and do not yet know angel ways," said Raziel.

"For what purpose were they created?" an angel asked.

Raziel drew a deep breath. "Satan is creating new mischief on earth," she said.

The angels shuddered at mention of the name of the former angel who, along with his followers, had been cast out of Heaven for insolence.

"What new mischief can there be?" asked an angel. "Already he has spread jealousy, greed, stealing, telling lies—"

"He has found a new outlet for the Evil Urge," Raziel said.

"Ohhh," the angels said, exchanging glances.

They felt sorry for the Holy One. He had made humans with two urges: one to do good, the other to do evil. Two—to give humans a choice. He hoped they would choose good and walk in his ways, and so draw closer to him. It always disappointed him to learn about evil acts on earth.

"Let's hope Satan is foiled," the inquiring angel said, and flew off. The other angels remained.

"This new mischief—how did it become known?" asked one.

"The Holy One heard cries and weeping, and sent Layla, Angel of the Night, to investigate."

"And?" the angels asked.

"Humans create for themselves houses to live in, roads to walk on, parks to play in," said Raziel.

"All good things," said an angel. "Where is the harm?"

"All good," Raziel repeated. "But there is danger where they work. They must put up signs reading DAN-GER, warning passersby to keep away."

It did not surprise her to see confusion on the faces of the angels. Heaven was all peace, harmony, love. The idea of danger was unknown to them.

"A sign—we know what that is," said an angel. "The marvels and wonders that the Holy One created on earth are signs of his greatness."

"He put together in one Heaven the sun, which is fire, and clouds, which are water," said another. "A sign that nothing is too difficult for him."

"He makes the sun sink gradually, giving fieldworkers and travelers time to reach home before dark—a sign of his compassion," said a third.

"The sign of which I speak is different," said Raziel. "It is an object, a flat surface with writing on it."

"We know writing," said another. "The shelves of Ya'asriel, Angel-of-the-Seventy-Pencils, and his assistants are filled with writing. But this other word—*danger*—what is it?" the angel asked.

Raziel knew that would be difficult to explain. She saw Angel Layla glide over to the new class of angels, to train them. "Layla has come to teach the newcomers," she said. "Go and listen, and you will learn what danger is."

The angels glanced up and saw the newcomers draw their hands in under their wings.

They flew over to the group.

"You have been created for the purpose of saving lives," Layla said to the newcomers.

The new angels swelled with pride.

"The Holy One has put waters between the lands on earth," Layla continued. "Humans drink some waters. In some, they find food. In others, they swim—it is a pastime they are fond of."

An angel who had come to listen giggled. "The seas are so full of fish. Is there room for humans?"

"The seas are vast," Layla said, "wide and deep—very wide and very deep. And they have currents," she continued. "Many kinds of fish live there. Among them are very large fish that favor human flesh."

"Uhhh," an angel said with a shudder.

"People who enter such waters can come to harm. It is the custom, therefore, to put up signs reading DANGER, warning them to stay away."

"It is a good thing," said an angel.

"It is," said Layla. "But Satan and his followers have turned this good to evil. They stir up the Evil Urge in a grudge-holder. When that person sees someone he hates near a place of danger, the Evil Urge whispers in his ear, 'Remove the DANGER sign.'"

The information unsettled the angels.

"It can also happen," said Layla, "that foolish people, to provoke foolish laughter, remove a sign. Or that a poorly made sign falls."

"There is work to be done," a newcomer angel said.

"You have been created to do the work," Layla said. "As Sign-Minders, you will patrol the earth, keeping an eye out for danger, and do what needs to be done."

The newcomers were moved by the thought that the Holy One cares for his humans. Their hearts swelled with a feeling of love. As if they had always been in Heaven and were familiar with songs of praise, they sang out, *"Holy, holy, holy is the Lord."*

"Go down now," said Layla. "Change yourselves into laborers, lifeguards, carpenters, haulers of wood or water, winds—whatever is needed to keep a life safe."

The newcomers flew off.

The listening angels hastened to a Leisure Corner of Heaven for a good view of earth, to see better how danger works. Where a pipe was being laid in a torn up street, they saw someone remove a DANGER sign. They saw a Sign-Minder, dressed as a laborer, return the sign to its place and secure it. Where a new road was being laid, someone had painted over a DANGER sign. A Sign-Minder in overalls removed the paint and restored the letters of the sign.

Sign-Minders were kept busy replacing old signs, putting up new ones, freshening faded letters, facing the right way signs that had been turned backward, digging up signs hidden in the sand. The watching angels saw a Sign-Minder turn himself into a wind and blow to safety a passerby who was about to fall into a pit.

They flew back to speak to Raziel. "We now know what danger is," said one.

"And what meanness humans are capable of," said another.

"Most humans are good," said Raziel. "But the ones who give in to the Evil Urge become mean."

A sound they had never heard before reached their ears.

"What is that?" asked an angel.

Raziel knew what it was. The Musician angels had returned from earth and were reproducing with their lips the musical sound they had brought back. She found the sound unpleasant and did not think it suited songs of praise.

"What is the name of this instrument?" she asked one of the returning Musician angels.

"They call it a tambourine," he said. "It is a sound for dancing."

From behind the Holy Curtain, a voice said, "Angels do not dance."

Angel laughter rippled through Heaven. Angels roll and leap, glide and tumble, hover and fly—but they cannot dance.

Raziel sensed the Holy One's pleasure. The sound of angel laughter was as dear, as precious to him as the sweetest song of praise.

A Trial in Heaven

"A broken heart is very dear and precious to God."
—RABBI NACHMAN OF BRESLOV

⁓

As Heaven rang with the sweet voices of the Choir singing *"Before the mountains were brought forth, before you formed the earth and the world, from everlasting to everlasting, you are God,"* the Holy One noticed among gliding and floating angels a band of angels with sad faces. A sad face was not a usual sight in Heaven.

"Come forward, little ones," he said.

Heads lowered, huddling together, the angels drifted through the amber precincts of Heaven toward the Holy Curtain.

"Why are you sad?" the Holy One asked.

The angels, speaking with one voice, said, "We have nothing to do and feel useless."

The answer surprised the Holy One. These angels were Guardians. They were among the busiest angels. He had created a Guardian for every living thing on earth. Each blade of grass had a Guardian of its own, telling it how to grow. Why did these sad-looking angels have nothing to do?

"How can you feel useless when you look after the welfare of . . . of . . ."

There were so many Guardian classes, the Holy One could not always recall which angels were Guardians of what.

"The dodo bird," the angels said helpfully.

"Yes, the dodo bird. Why would you feel useless?" the Holy One said.

The angels shuffled uneasily. "We . . . they . . . there . . . ," they stammered, finding it hard to say more.

Angel Raziel knew their story and spoke for them. "They feel useless because the dodo has disappeared, and they have no work," she said.

The angels bowed their heads, sorry to be the cause of bad news. The Holy One loved each and every creature he had made. And now an entire species was gone. They also felt bad for themselves. They had been devoted Guardians and had tried by all means possible to save the dodo—but without success.

"If the bird has disappeared, we must learn why," the Holy One said.

The Guardians felt uneasy. They thought they would be reassigned, and that would be that. They didn't think there would be an inquiry.

"Let the Heavenly Court be convened," the Holy One said.

A trial! The Guardians were stricken. They never expected this. Their hope was to keep the details of the dodo's disappearance sealed behind their lips. At a trial they would have to answer questions, be forced to say things they had no wish to say, things it pained them even to think in the privacy of their minds.

The call was out. News spreads quickly in Heaven. From every direction angel Judges began arriving to take their places, three from each class—Wheels, Lights, Winds, Guardians, Seraphim, Cherubim, Singers, Destroyers, Flames, Scribes, Healers, Lawyers, and all the others. Angels whose duties were over for the day called to each other, "Come and see," and floated into the Court to listen.

The sight of the assembled Judges unnerved the Guardians.

"Raziel, let the matter begin."

The Holy One spoke from behind the Holy Curtain.

Following rules, Raziel called, "A trial cannot commence without an accuser. Is there an accuser?"

From the Lawyer section arose a certain Lawyer angel always willing—no, eager—to accuse.

Coming forward, facing the Guardians, he said, "I accuse you."

Fear and nervousness overtook the Guardians. They did not know where to look. He would pull from them answers they did not want to give. With linked minds, thinking as one, they cried, "We are guilty!" seeking to end the idea of a trial.

Raziel found their behavior strange. "You cannot judge yourselves," she told them. "The accuser must first question you. The Judges here assembled will then decide if you are innocent or guilty."

The accuser glanced at the angel Judges, then turned to the Guardians.

"The court has been told you have done everything that could be done for the dodo," the accuser said.

"So we have," the angels said.

"Yet the dodo has disappeared. How do you account for that?"

The angels were silent.

"You must answer," Raziel said kindly.

A stony silence filled the court. The angels loved the Holy One. To speak the truth—and there was no other kind of answer in Heaven—would be a terrible and hurtful thing.

"Well?" said the accuser.

"You must answer," Raziel repeated.

All eyes were on the Guardians. They had no choice but to speak. Squirming, twisting, their hearts breaking for having to say what had to be said, they forced from their lips the painful words, "The dodo was poorly made."

A gasp went up in the court.

So that is why they did not want a trial, Raziel thought. *They did not want to point out a flaw in the Holy One's handiwork.*

The accuser turned to the Judges. "You have heard them: 'The dodo was poorly made,'" he said in mocking tones. "Therefore, the disappearance of the dodo was not their fault." He glanced from angel face to angel face. "If it wasn't their fault, whose fault was it?"

The Guardians turned crimson with embarrassment.

"If it was not their fault, as they allege," the accuser continued, "it was, ipso facto, the fault of the Creator, the one who gives life and takes it away."

The angels whimpered with distress and were on the point of collapse.

The accuser turned back to them. "Tell the Court why you think the dodo bird was poorly made," he said.

The angels said nothing.

"Did the bird have eyes to see with?"

"It did," they answered with a quavering voice.

"Did it have a beak to eat with?"

"It did."

"Did it have legs to move from one place to another?"

"The legs were there," the angels said weakly.

"And wings? As birds, they had wings, did they not?"

The Guardians cringed.

"Did it have ears to hear with, as you do?" the accuser said, mocking their silence.

Laughter arose in the court.

"Please answer," Raziel said.

Biting their lips, trembling, the angels said softly, "That was the problem—the wings. They were too small."

Surprised gasps went up in the court.

"Are you wing experts?" the accuser asked.

The Judges laughed. Raziel covered her mouth, to laugh with them.

"Tell the Court why you think the wings were too small," the accuser said.

"The dodo was a big bird, and heavy," the Guardian angels said. "Too heavy to lift itself off the ground—or flee—when danger came."

"Each Guardian is given miracles to perform, for a time of need," the accuser said. "Weren't you also given miracles to use?"

"We were given one miracle," the angels said.

"And that was . . . ?"

"We were given the power to toss up bushes where there were none."

"Tell the Court how this worked," the accuser said.

The angels answered, "When we saw a dodo in trouble, we tossed up a bush for the bird to hide behind. But the dodo was greedy for food. As fast as we tossed up a bush, the dodo ate it. They ate their hiding places. That is how they disappeared."

"You could have asked for a second miracle," the accuser said. "Heaven is not stingy with its miracles."

"We did not want to bother Heaven," the angels said.

The accuser looked at the Judges. "Did the dodo disappear because it was poorly made? Or did the Guardians do a poor job?" he said.

The angels were frightened but could not let the accuser have the last word. "We did our best," they said.

"You did your best poorly," the accuser said.

"What more could we have done?" the angels asked.

"You could have tossed up bigger bushes," the accuser said.

"That was the bush size we were given," said the angels.

"You could have tossed up less tasty bushes."

"That was the type of bush we were given," the Guardians said.

The accuser turned to the Court. "Angels are resourceful and inventive," he said. "These Guardians were neither. It is their fault and no one else's that the dodo has disappeared."

From behind the Holy Curtain the Holy One said, "It is not their fault."

Silence gripped the courtroom. The words stunned the angels.

"The dodo birds were lazy," the Holy One said. "I

did not make them that way. Nor did I make them heavy. They had eyes to see with and ears to hear with. They were equipped to recognize danger. If they had eaten less, they would have been able to run from danger. If they had exercised and strengthened their wings, they would have been able to fly. Others of my creatures have found ways to outwit attackers. It is the fault of the dodoes themselves that they have disappeared."

"O Holy One!" the accused angels cried softly, faint with love.

Raziel faced the Judges. "Have you reached a verdict?"

"The angels are innocent," the Judges said with one voice.

Judgment had been rendered. The trial was over. The soft murmur of angel talk and tinkling angel laughter filled Heaven as the accuser slunk away.

In their joy to be found innocent, the Guardians stood hugging and kissing each other. But the feeling of uselessness soon crept over them again. They were still Guardians without a creature to guard, without a link to earth.

The Holy One knew their thoughts. "I have seen how the accuser pulled from you answers you did not wish to release," he said. "And how it broke your hearts to speak words that you thought would be hurtful to me."

The angels were on the point of tears with gratitude.

"A broken heart is very dear to me," he said. "I see the need for a new group of Guardians," the Holy One said.

Curious, the Guardians waited to hear more.

"Gabriel," the Holy One called.

The Archangel appeared.

"I have created a Guardian for every plant, for every brook, for every creature, for every human, but not broken hearts," the Holy One said. "Instruct Ya'asriel, Angel-of-the-Seventy-Pencils, to open a book for a new group of angels—Guardians of Broken Hearts. And let him enter on the first page the story of these good angels."

"O Holy One!" the angels said, overflowing with gratitude.

Gabriel drifted off to the workshop of the scribe.

"You are now Guardians of people with broken hearts," the Holy One said. "There are many of them. Seek them out and console them, comfort them and show them hope."

The angels were so happy and grateful, they became confused and did not know how to proceed.

"What shall we do?" they asked Raziel.

"Collect your miracle at the gate," she said. "And by the way," she added, "the accuser was right about one thing. Heaven is not stingy with its miracles. Don't be shy to ask."

The angels started for the gate. But as the Choir began a new round of praise, they could not bring themselves to leave. They were overflowing with love for the Holy One and wanted to sing. Oh, how they wanted to sing!

They waited for the Choir to finish the introduction, then joined the singers lustily and with a full heart—

"He is great, and his works are great.
Hallelujah, hallelu!"

Palace of Love

"God exchanges kisses with his souls in the Palace of Love."
—Zohar, the Book of Splendor

⁓

Heaven filled with the sweet murmur of angel talk and the soft brush of wing meeting wing as angels passed one another, changing stations. Outside the Holy Curtain, Raziel sat idly enjoying the pleasant sounds when the gatekeeper of the Palace of Love, the dwelling place of souls, approached the Curtain to speak to the Holy One. That could mean only one thing: there was trouble in the palace.

"Holy One—" the gatekeeper began.

"Again?" said the Holy One before the gatekeeper could say more.

"Again," said the gatekeeper.

"The same soul?" asked the Holy One.

"The same," said the gatekeeper.

A sigh came from behind the Holy Curtain.

The Holy One loves his souls and they love him. But sometimes their love takes an unwelcome form. Now and then, when he sends for a soul, to place it in the body of a newborn, the soul refuses. It does not want to leave Heaven and be separated from the amber rays of Glory, the nearness of the Holy One.

"I let it pass the last time," the Holy One said. "I cannot do so again. It could set a pattern."

Rafael, Angel-of-Cures-and-Remedies, appeared at the Holy Curtain with a writing pad. "I am here for the lesson of the day, Holy One," Rafael said.

The Holy One first spoke to the gatekeeper. "Return to the palace," he said. "I will be along soon to deal with the problem."

The gatekeeper turned and left.

"What shall I learn today, Holiness?" Rafael asked, the pad open before him.

"Wisdom is revealed through the carob, the palm, and the pistachio trees," the Holy One said.

Rafael wrote down the words. "Holy One," he said, looking up, "which part of the tree would that be? Leaves? Fruit? Bark? And the wisdom, how is it to be passed on? As a liquid to be drunk? A solid to be eaten or swallowed? Something to be inhaled? A cream to be spread?"

"That is for you and your assistants to determine," the Holy One said. "Examine the parts, find the essence, extract and distill its properties. Your findings will guide you."

Rafael bowed. "I will assign angels to study the named trees and report back to you what we find," he said.

"I already know what you will find," the Holy One said.

Raziel tried to keep from laughing. Of course the Holy One knew. He had created the trees.

"I meant," Rafael said, embarrassed, "I will let you know, to see if our findings are correct."

"Very well," the Holy One said.

When it grew silent, Raziel knew that the conversation was over and that the Holy One had turned toward the Palace of Love.

All angels knew of the existence of the palace, but none knew where in the vastness of Heaven it was located. Raziel and the archangels knew it was located in a corner of the Garden of Eden but did not know where the garden was.

The Holy One often visited the Palace of Love to enjoy the company of the souls he created. He was the source of their happiness, the amber light of Glory, filling all heavens everywhere at all times.

One night, sensing the presence of the Holy One, souls came gliding and floating excitedly from all directions. As the Holy One was exchanging pleasantries with each soul, giving each one equal attention, he noticed one soul sulking in a far corner.

"Come to me, little one. Let us talk together."

The soul knew what to expect. "I cannot bear to be away from you," he cried softly.

"All the souls I put into the bodies of newborn infants enter willingly," said the Holy One.

Flecks of unhappiness mottled the soul. "I know," the soul said, twisting and turning. "But I love you...."

"If you love me, you will fulfill the purpose I made you for," the Holy One said.

The soul whimpered.

"I created links between my worlds, to bring Heaven closer to my humans and my humans closer to Heaven. When you refuse to be a link, you work against my plan."

"Perhaps I am deficient," the soul said.

"I did not make you deficient," said the Holy One.

"Then I am weak."

"A weak soul would not be able to perform the hard tasks souls are assigned to carry out," the Holy One said.

"I know," the soul said. "To help a person to be good, keep a person from doing a wrong and harmful thing—"

"Yes," said the Holy One.

"That is not always easy," the soul said.

"It is not always easy for me to control my souls either," the Holy One said.

The soul wrinkled with shame.

"Look about yourself. What do you see?" the Holy One said.

The soul glanced about. "I see thousands of souls, some waiting to be assigned to bodies, some resting here between assignments, some arriving from the workshop of Ya'asriel, Angel-of-the-Seventy-Pencils."

"And what have they done there?"

"They have left sleeping the bodies they occupy and gone to report the person's doings to the scribe in charge of the Book of Deeds."

"And then?"

"Then they come here, to the Palace of Love, to be with you before returning to their bodies."

"Then they are here each night?" the Holy One said.

"Each night," the soul repeated.

"Then no soul is ever parted from Heaven for very long," the Holy One said.

The soul brightened. "I have been foolish, Holy One," said the soul.

"Not foolish, just looking with closed eyes," said the Holy One. "Come, an infant is about to be born. I will slip you into its body."

The Holy One kissed the soul and sent it on its way.

⌣

Again and again, one soul or another doesn't want to be separated from Heaven and the Glory of the Holy One. And always and always, the matter ends with a few sweet words and a kiss.

Sources and References

I have drawn upon the Hebrew Bible, Louis Ginzberg's classic *Legends of the Bible* (New York: Simon and Schuster, 1956), and the sources cited below.

INTRODUCTION

In the Kabbalah, the book of Jewish mysticism, the angel Raziel is characterized as possessing divine wisdom. Mystical texts speak of wisdom in the feminine.

Glatzer, Nahum N., ed. *Hammer on the Rock, A Short Midrash Reader.* Translated by Jacob Sloan. New York: Schocken Books, 1948.

Luzzatto, Moshe Chaim. *The Way of God.* Translated by Aryeh Kaplan. New York: Feldheim, 1998.

ANGELS OF FORGETFULNESS

Luzzatto, Moshe Chaim. *The Way of God.* Translated by Aryeh Kaplan. New York: Feldheim, 1998.

Scholem, Gershom, ed. *Zohar, the Book of Splendor: Basic Readings from the Kabbalah.* New York: Schocken Books, 1995.

Weiner, Jonathan. *Time, Love, Memory: A Great Biologist and His Quest for the Origins of Behavior.* New York: Knopf, 1999.

ALPHABET ANGELS

Buber, Martin. *Tales of the Hasidim*. Translated by Olga Marx. New York: Schocken Books, 1991.

Epstein, Perle. *Kabbalah: The Way of the Jewish Mystic*. Garden City, NY: Doubleday, 1978.

Frankl, Walter. *Israel Gardening Encyclopedia: Month by Month*. Jerusalem: Carta and The Jerusalem Post, 1981.

STAY, STONE, STAY

A Jewish folktale-type story written by the author to accompany the other angel stories.

SIGN-MINDERS

Bialik, Hayim Nahman, and Yehoshua Hana Ravnitzky, eds. *The Book of Legends: Legends from the Talmud and Midrash*. Translated by William G. Braude. New York: Schocken Books, 1992.

Isaacson, Ben. *Dictionary of the Jewish Religion*. Edited by David C. Gross. New York: Bantam Books, 1979.

Luzzatto, Moshe Chaim. *The Way of God*. Translated by Aryeh Kaplan. New York: Feldheim, 1998.

A TRIAL IN HEAVEN

Luzzatto, Moshe Chaim. *The Way of God*. Translated by Aryeh Kaplan. New York: Feldheim, 1998.

PALACE OF LOVE

Covitz, Joel. *Visions of the Night: A Study of Jewish Dream Interpretation*. Boston: Shambhala, 1990.

Luzzatto, Moshe Chaim. *The Way of God*. Translated by Aryeh Kaplan. New York: Feldheim, 1998.

Runes, Dagobert D., ed. *The Wisdom of the Kabbalah, as Represented by Chapters Taken from the Book Zohar*. Translated by S. L. MacGregor Mathers. New York: Citadel Press, 1967.

Scholem, Gershom, ed. *Zohar, the Book of Splendor: Basic Readings from the Kabbalah*. New York: Schocken Books, 1995.